The Family Who Won A Million

& Other Family Stories

Compiled by Alison Sage

Illustrated by Tony Ross

A Red Fox Book

Published by Random House Children's Books
20 Vauxhall Bridge Road, London SW1V 2SA

A division of Random House UK Ltd
London Melbourne Sydney Auckland
Johannesburg and agencies throughout the world

Copyright © in this collection Alison Sage 1996
Copyright © illustrations Tony Ross 1996
Copyright © text individual authors

First published in Great Britain by
Hutchinson Children's Books 1996

Red Fox edition 1997

3 5 7 9 10 8 6 4 2

Printed and bound in Great Britain by
Cox & Wyman Ltd, Reading, Berkshire

RANDOM HOUSE UK Limited Reg. No. 954009

Papers used by Random House UK Limited
are natural, recyclable products made from wood grown in
sustainable forests. The manufacturing processes conform to
the environmental regulations of the country of origin.

ISBN 0 09 966871 8

With Compliments

Contents

The Family Who Won a Million

Caroline Castle

The key turned in the lock. We froze, all four of us. My cousin, dopey Janine, grabbed my shirt and made a high-pitched whiny noise like a hamster being strangled. We'd known that time was getting on, but somehow we'd just got carried away with the game. It had started out as 'chuck the trainer' and ended up as 'chuck anything you can put your hands on'.

Mum fell through the door, dropping a hundredweight of Tesco bags. A super-economy bottle of Major Brights All Purpose Lemon detergent rolled across the floor and bumped with a watery flop against my trainer. Unfortunately, it wasn't on my foot at the time. Janine stared at it as if it was the most interesting thing she had ever witnessed; Richard, my other cousin, sidled into the kitchen and began to straighten Mum's favourite picture, 'Mimosia, an Island Paradise', which was about to fall off the wall. And my sister Rachel suddenly needed to see to Podge, the baby, who couldn't understand why he had to be brutally woken in the middle of a blissful sleep to have a perfectly clean nappy changed. My brother Jake had gone to football practice.

This, as so often happens, left me to face the music.

'Oh, no, no, *no!*' said Mum, surveying what looked like the War of the Oxfam Shops. 'This is really the end. You kids. What on earth has been going on here?'

'Sorry,' I mumbled, which wasn't going to get me anywhere, 'we were playing and . . .'

'Spare me,' said Mum. 'Just get it all cleared up, pronto. *I* will make the tea and I want it spic-and-span by the time I've finished. Fifteen minutes. Do you hear me?'

As she took off her jacket, a flimsy piece of pink paper fell from her pocket and floated to the floor. I picked it up. It was our lottery ticket. We had bought a ticket every week since it started, but so far we had won absolutely nothing, zilch! I handed it to Mum.

'What numbers did you choose this time?' asked Rachel.

For a moment Mum looked dreamy and far away. 'All your birthdays,' she said. Then her smile faded. 'But it'll be all your yesterdays, unless you get moving!'

'When we win, we can get a cleaner,' I grumbled, picking up the contents of my school bag that were scattered through the hall.

At that moment, the Podge, tired of being ignored, let out an ear-piercing screech and bit Rachel's leg. She fell sideways and knocked over the jam jar full of pencils.

'If we win,' sighed Mum in her I'm-too-tired-to-be-angry voice, 'I'm going to buy a rocket and blast you all off to the Planet Hooliganamus, where I'm sure you'll all feel right at home.'

*

This was life at 15a Barkingside or, as Mum often called it, Barkingmad, Terrace. It hadn't been too bad until Janine and Richard had come to live with us. Auntie Sara had just dumped them on us, saying, 'It'll only be for a few days, Sis. Opportunity of a lifetime. I've got three songs – the biggest nightclub in Bradford!' That was two months ago and they were still here. Janine squashed into the bedroom with me and Rachel, and *sharing my clothes*, would you believe? And Mum having to spend Rachel's trainer money on new stuff for Richard, who hadn't spoken a word since Auntie Sara left. If this wasn't enough, a gang of Hell's Angels had moved in upstairs who played heavy metal all day long and sounded as if they were tap dancing in gum boots. I don't know how I coped.

Well, after we'd cleaned up, we all sat round telling Mum the things we needed and the things that needed doing. As usual, she wasn't listening, but was clearing stuff away at high speed in a sort of manic trance, stopping every few minutes to wipe the Podge's nose.

'And another thing,' I said, glaring at my loathsome cousins. 'Why are they still here? I want our room back! *And* I haven't got any clothes left.'

Mum turned on me and gave me a look that would fell Godzilla's big brother at a hundred paces.

'Janine and Richard are welcome *as long as they*

need to stay,' she said. 'And if you weren't such a selfish little madam, and *just thought* for a minute, you might just understand what it must be like for them too.'

'And what about my trainers?' said Rachel, ignoring Mum. 'OK, I said I'd wait, but for how much longer, eh? By the time I get them they'll be antiques.'

At that moment my brother Jake burst into the kitchen, his hand clasped to his right eye, which we could see had turned a violent combination of black and blue.

'What on earth . . .?' said Mum.

'Nigel Pring,' said Jake, matter of factly. 'He punched me in the face. He said our computer's rubbish.'

'Shouldn't you be the one to punch him?' said Rachel.

'No, Rachel, love,' sighed Mum. 'People'd just as soon get at you for what you haven't got, as what you have.'

At that moment Janine whinged, '*When's* our mum coming back?' and burst into tears.

'Can we get a new computer?' said Jake. 'With a CD ROM. Everyone's got one, 'cept us. Nigel Pring is on the Internet.'

'Give me strength,' said Mum.

I couldn't sleep that night. Not only was Janine

snoring but the Hell's Angels were playing something that sounded like a road drill in an echo chamber. Heaven knows how the others slept through it.

I wandered, bleary eyed, into the kitchen. Mum was still up, the Podge slumped across her lap looking like the angel he never was, and never would be, in waking life. It was stifling hot, and Mum suddenly looked very tired. She was staring intently at the wall.

'Hiya,' I said. 'What are you looking at?'

'That,' said Mum, pointing at the picture that had nearly seen its last that afternoon. 'Mimosia Island. Sand, blue, blue sea and . . . silence.'

On cue, almost miraculously, the road drill music stopped and for a moment we stepped into that other distant, peaceful world before a blast of something that sounded like a hundred hippopotamuses being tortured came ricocheting through our ceiling.

The next day, Saturday, we all had headaches. I was spending the day with my best friend Kate; Mum forced me to take dopey Janine saying, 'The two of you should try to get on more. Try to have some fun.' Some hope.

It was after eight when we got back to Barkingside Terrace. I noticed at once that something was up. For a start, the back door was open. Secondly, the strangest noises were coming from inside, a sort of screeching and yelling and crying and laughing all mixed together. 'What on earth has happened?' I said, walking into the lounge to find everyone rolling about suffering from some sort of mass hysteria.

Rachel's face was red and shining. 'Oh, Hannah!' she cried. 'You'll never guess . . . You'll never guess in a *million billion zillion* years.' She was waving a small piece of paper about. A small piece of flimsy pink paper. I hardly dared breathe.

'We've *won*,' she screeched, clasping me in a bear hug. 'We've only gone and won the lottery! Imagine, all our birthdays!'

The next day, when everyone had calmed down enough to stay still for more than ten seconds, we all sat round the table grinning like idiots. We had found out that six other people had the same numbers, but our share was *a million pounds*. A million pounds! It was fantastic, incredible!

'Well,' said Rachel, 'no need to wait for my trainers now! I can get a whole *wardrobe* of trainers; one pair in every colour! One pair for every week of the year; a different pair for every day of the week!'

'And as soon as I get my new computer,' said Jake, 'I'm going right up to Nigel Pring and I'm going to punch him in the face and tell him his is rubbish.'

'And I'm going to get . . .' I said, not quite sure as a multitude of treasures – clothes, roller skates, a swimming pool, a great shining chauffeur-driven car – swam around my brain in glorious technicolour.

'In any case,' I went on, 'we can get a new house. *A great big house*, and I can have my own room with my *own telly.*'

'No,' said Mum.

'No!' we all said, astonished.

Mum looked strange. Distant and far away.

'No,' she said quietly. 'No computers, no trainers, no tellys, no big houses or cars.'

'What do you mean?' said Rachel, looking worried. For a moment we all looked like goldfish out of water, our mouths open, gaping for air. The same ghastly thought went through our minds: had Mum gone mad? Was she going to give it all away to some dogs' home or something? Or maybe she really was going to buy that rocket . . .

'Mimosia,' she said softly.

'Mimosia?' we all repeated like a load of brainless parrots.

'Mimosia,' she said again, looking up at her beloved picture. 'We're going to pack our suitcases, close up the house, get on an aeroplane and walk straight into that glorious calm, blue afternoon, just as I've done a million times in my dreams.'

I'm watching Richard and Janine. They're sitting on the sand right on the edge of the tide with their feet in the blue-green water. I'm under the tree, as usual, because I can't take the sun, not for long anyway. I'm writing my diary . . . writing, writing . . .

I haven't stopped since it all happened. It's important to get it down, in case I forget.

I've never seen Mum happier. She found us this house, right on the beach and now we all live here, Mum, Rachel, me, Jake, the Podge, Janine, Richard, and even Auntie Sara, who arrived last week full of presents and apologies. Mum had left our new address with next door, and Auntie Sarah just flew right out. 'Opportunity of a lifetime,' she said, sweeping Janine and Rich off the floor in a great big hug. It's hard to believe, I know, but slowly they turned into normal human beings. Richard started talking again and Janine, well, she's really OK.

I'm finishing now, closing the book. The sun is setting – a great big orange planet sinking into the sea.

Jake is running up from the tide and flops down beside me. 'Ha!' he laughs, rolling over in the sand. 'If only Nigel Pring could see me now!'

Sometimes we miss the telly and the computer and sometimes we dream about all the things we never got, like the car and the swimming pool.

But you can't have everything, can you – even when you've got a million pounds!

The Family Dog

Judy Blume

I learned to stand on my head in gym class. I'm pretty good at it too. I can stay up for as long as three minutes. I showed my mother, my father and Fudge how I can do it right in the living room. They were all impressed. Especially Fudge. He wanted to do it too. So I turned him upside down and tried to teach him. But he always tumbled over backwards.

Right after I learned to stand on my head Fudge stopped eating. He did it suddenly. One day he ate fine and the next day nothing. 'No eat!' he told my mother.

She didn't pay too much attention to him until the third day. When he still refused to eat she got upset. 'You've got to eat, Fudgie,' she said. 'You want to grow up to be big and strong, don't you?'

'No grow!' Fudge said.

That night my mother told my father how worried she was about Fudge. So my father did tricks for him while my mother stood over his chair trying to get some food into his mouth. But nothing worked. Not even juggling oranges.

Finally my mother got the brilliant idea of me standing on my head while she fed Fudge. I wasn't very excited about standing on my head in the kitchen. The floor is awfully hard in there. But my mother begged me. She said, 'It's very important for Fudge to eat. Please help us, Peter.'

So I stood on my head. When Fudge saw me upside down he clapped his hands and laughed. When he laughs he opens his mouth. That's when my mother stuffed some baked potato into it.

But the next morning I put my foot down. 'No! I don't want to stand on my head in the kitchen. Or anywhere else!' I added, 'And if I don't hurry I'll be late for school.'

'Don't you care if your brother starves?'

'No!' I told her.

'Peter! What an awful thing to say.'

'Oh . . . he'll eat when he gets hungry. Why don't you just leave him alone!'

That afternoon when I came home from school I found my brother on the kitchen floor playing with boxes of cereals and raisins and dried apricots. My mother was begging him to eat.

'No, no, no!' Fudge shouted. He made a terrible mess, dumping everything on the floor.

'Please stand on your head, Peter,' my mother said. 'It's the only way he'll eat.'

'No!' I told her. 'I'm not going to stand on my head any more.' I went into my room and slammed the door. I played with Dribble until supper-time. Nobody ever worries about me the way they worry about Fudge. If I decided not to eat they'd probably never even notice!

That night during dinner Fudge hid under the kitchen table. He said, 'I'm a doggie. Woof . . . woof . . . woof!'

It was hard to eat with him under the table pulling on my legs. I waited for my father to say something. But he didn't.

Finally my mother jumped up. 'I know,' she said. 'If Fudgie's a doggie he wants to eat on the floor! Right?'

17

If you ask me Fudge never even thought about that. But he liked the idea a lot. He barked and nodded his head. So my mother fixed his plate and put it under the table. Then she reached down and petted him, like he was a real dog.

My father said, 'Aren't we carrying this a little too far?'

My mother didn't answer.

Fudge ate two bites of his dinner.

My mother was satisfied.

After a week of having him eat under the table I felt like we really did have a family dog. I thought how great it would be if we could trade in Fudge for a nice cocker spaniel. That would solve all my problems. I'd walk him and feed him and play with him. He could even sleep on the edge of my bed at night. But of course that was wishful thinking. My brother is here to stay. And there's nothing much I can do about it.

Grandma came over with a million ideas about getting Fudge to eat. She tricked him by making milk shakes in the blender. When Fudge wasn't looking she threw in an egg. Then she told him if he drank it all up there would be a surprise in the bottom of the glass. The first time he believed her. He finished his milk shake. But all he saw was an empty glass. There wasn't any surprise! Fudge got so mad he threw the glass down. It smashed into little pieces. After that Grandma left.

The next day my mother dragged Fudge to Dr Cone's office. He told her to leave him alone. That Fudge would eat when he got hungry.

I reminded my mother that I'd told her the same thing – and for free! But I guess my mother didn't believe either one of us because she took Fudge to see three more doctors. None of them could find a thing wrong with my brother. One doctor even suggested that my mother cook Fudge his favourite foods.

So that night my mother broiled lamb chops just for Fudge. The rest of us ate stew. She served him the two little lamb chops on his plate under the table. Just the smell of them was enough to make my stomach growl. I thought it was mean of my mother to make them for Fudge and not for me.

Fudge looked at his lamb chops for a few minutes. Then he pushed his plate away. 'No!' he said. 'No chops!'

'Fudgie . . . you'll starve!' my mother cried. 'You *must* eat!'

'No chops! Corn flakes,' Fudge said. 'Want corn flakes!'

My mother ran to get the cereal for Fudge. 'You can eat the chops if you want them, Peter,' she told me.

I reached down and helped myself to the lamb chops. My mother handed Fudge his bowl of cereal. But he didn't eat it. He sat at my feet and looked up at me. He watched me eat his chops.

'*Eat your cereal!*' my father said.

'NO! NO EAT CEREAL!' Fudge yelled.

My father was really mad. His face turned bright red. He said, 'Fudge, you will eat that cereal or you will wear it!'

This was turning out to be fun after all, I thought. And the lamb chops were really tasty. I dipped the bone in some ketchup and chewed away.

Fudge messed around with his cereal for a minute. Then he looked at my father and said, 'NO EAT . . . NO EAT . . . NO EAT!'

My father wiped his mouth with his napkin, pushed back his chair, and got up from the table. He picked up the bowl of cereal in one hand, and Fudge in the other. He carried them both into the bathroom. I went along, nibbling on a bone, to see what was going to happen.

My father stood Fudge in the bath and dumped the whole bowl of cereal right over his head. Fudge screamed. He sure can scream loud.

My father motioned for me to go back to the kitchen. He joined us in a minute. We sat down and finished our dinner. Fudge kept on screaming. My mother wanted to go to him but my father told her to stay where she was. He'd had enough of Fudge's monkey business at meal times.

I think my mother really was relieved that my father had taken over. For once my brother got what he deserved. And I was glad!

The next day Fudge sat at the table again. In his little red booster chair, where he belongs. He ate everything my mother put in front of him. 'No more doggie,' he told us.

And for a long time after that his favourite expression was 'eat it or wear it'!

Nothing to Be Afraid Of

Jan Mark

'Robin won't give you any trouble,' said Auntie Lynn. 'He's very quiet.'

Anthea knew how quiet Robin was. At present he was sitting under the table and, until Auntie Lynn mentioned his name, she had forgotten that he was there.

Auntie Lynn put a carrier bag on the armchair.

'There's plenty of clothes, so you won't need to do any washing, and there's a spare pair of pyjamas in case – well, you know. In case . . .'

'Yes,' said Mum, firmly. 'He'll be all right. I'll ring you tonight and let you know how he's getting along.' She looked at the clock. 'Now, hadn't *you* better be getting along?'

She saw Auntie Lynn to the front door and Anthea heard them saying good-bye to each other. Mum almost told Auntie Lynn to stop worrying and have a good time, which would have been a mistake because Auntie Lynn was going up North to a funeral.

Auntie Lynn was not really an Aunt, but she had once been at school with Anthea's mum, and she was the kind of person who couldn't manage without a handle to her name; so Robin was not Anthea's cousin. Robin was not anything much, except four years old, and he looked a lot younger; probably because nothing ever happened to him. Auntie Lynn kept no pets that might give Robin germs, and never bought him toys that had sharp corners to dent him or wheels that could be swallowed. He wore balaclava helmets and bobble hats in winter to protect his tender ears, and a knitted vest under his shirt in summer in case he overheated himself and caught a chill from his own sweat.

'Perspiration,' said Auntie Lynn.

His face was as pale and flat as a saucer of milk, and his eyes floated in it like drops of cod-liver oil. This was not so surprising as he was full to the back teeth with cod-liver oil; also with extract of malt, concentrated orange juice and calves-foot jelly. When you picked him up you expected him to squelch, like a hot-water bottle full of half-set custard.

Anthea lifted the tablecloth and looked at him.

'Hello, Robin.'

Robin stared at her with his flat eyes and went back to sucking his woolly doggy that had flat eyes also, of sewn-on felt, because glass ones might find their way into Robin's appendix and cause damage. Anthea wondered how long it would be before he noticed that his mother had gone. Probably he wouldn't, any more than he would notice when she came back.

Mum closed the front door and joined Anthea in looking under the table at Robin. Robin's mouth turned down at the corners, and Anthea hoped he would cry so that they could cuddle him. It seemed impolite to cuddle him before he needed it. Anthea was afraid to go any closer.

'What a little troll,' said Mum, sadly, lowering the tablecloth. 'I suppose he'll come out when he's hungry.'

Anthea doubted it.

Robin didn't want any lunch or any tea.

'Do you think he's pining?' said Mum. Anthea did not. Anthea had a nasty suspicion that he was like this all the time. He went to bed without making a fuss and fell asleep before the light was out, as if he were too bored to stay awake. Anthea left her bedroom door open, hoping that he would have a nightmare so that she could go in and comfort him, but Robin slept all night without a squeak, and woke in the morning as flat-faced as before. Wall-eyed Doggy looked more excitable than Robin did.

'If only we had a proper garden,' said Mum, as Robin went under the table again, leaving his breakfast eggs scattered round the plate. 'He might run about.'

Anthea thought that this was unlikely, and in any case they didn't have a proper garden, only a yard at the back and a stony strip in front, without a fence.

'Can I take him to the park?' said Anthea.

Mum looked doubtful. 'Do you think he wants to go?'

'No,' said Anthea, peering under the tablecloth.

'I don't think he wants to do anything, but he can't sit there all day.'

'I bet he can,' said Mum. 'Still, I don't think he should. All right, take him to the park, but keep quiet about it. I don't suppose Lynn thinks you're safe in traffic.'

'He might tell her.'

'Can he talk?'

Robin, still clutching wall-eyed Doggy, plodded beside her all the way to the park, without once trying to jam his head between the library railings or get run over by a bus.

'Hold my hand, Robin,' Anthea said as they left the house, and he clung to her like a lamprey.

The park was not really a park at all; it was a garden. It did not even pretend to be a park and the notice by the gate said KING STREET GARDENS, in case anyone tried to use it as a park. The grass was as green and as flat as the front-room carpet, but the front-room carpet had a path worn across it from the door to the fireplace, and here there were more notices that said KEEP OFF THE GRASS, so that the gritty white paths went obediently round the edge, under the orderly trees that stood in a row like the queue outside a fish shop. There were bushes in each corner and one shelter with a bench in it. Here and there brown holes in the grass, full of raked earth, waited for next year's flowers, but there were no flowers now, and the bench had been taken out of the shelter because the shelter was supposed to be a summer-house, and you couldn't have people using a summer-house in winter.

Robin stood by the gates and gaped, with Doggy depending limply from his mouth where he held it by one ear, between his teeth. Anthea decided that if they met anyone she knew, she would explain that Robin was only two, but very big for his age.

'Do you want to run, Robin?'

Robin shook his head.

'There's nothing to be afraid of. You can go all the way round, if you like, but you mustn't walk on the grass or pick things.'

Robin nodded. It was the kind of place that he understood.

Anthea sighed. 'Well, let's walk round, then.'

They set off. At each corner, where the bushes were, the path diverged. One part went in front of the bushes, one part round the back of them. On the first circuit Robin stumped glumly beside Anthea in front of the bushes. The second time round she felt a very faint tug at her hand. Robin wanted to go his own way.

This called for a celebration. Robin could think. Anthea crouched down on the path until they were at the same level.

'You want to walk round the back of the bushes,

Robin?'

'Yiss,' said Robin.

Robin could *talk*.

'All right, but listen.' She lowered her voice to a whisper. 'You must be very careful. That path is called Leopard Walk. Do you know what a leopard is?'

'Yiss.'

'There are two leopards down there. They live in the bushes. One is a good leopard and the other's a bad leopard. The good leopard has black spots. The bad leopard has red spots. If you see the bad leopard you must say, "Die leopard die or I'll kick you in the eye," and run like anything. Do you understand?'

Robin tugged again.

'Oh no,' said Anthea. 'I'm going *this* way. If you want to go down Leopard Walk, you'll have to go on your own. I'll meet you at the other end. Remember, if it's got red spots, run like mad.'

Robin trotted away. The bushes were just high enough to hide him, but Anthea could see the bobble on his hat doddering along. Suddenly the bobble gathered speed and Anthea had to run to reach the end of the bushes first.

'Did you see the bad leopard?'

'No,' said Robin, but he didn't look too sure.

'Why were you running, then?'

'I just wanted to.'

'You've dropped Doggy,' said Anthea. Doggy lay on the path with his legs in the air, halfway down Leopard Walk.

'You get him,' said Robin.

'No, *you* get him,' said Anthea. 'I'll wait here.' Robin moved off, reluctantly. She waited until he had recovered Doggy and then shouted, 'I can see the bad leopard in the bushes!' Robin raced back to safety. 'Did you say, "Die leopard die or I'll kick you in the eye"?' Anthea demanded.

'No,' Robin said, guiltily.

'Then he'll *kill* us,' said Anthea. 'Come on, run. We've got to get to that tree. He can't hurt us once we're under that tree.'

They stopped running under the twisted boughs of a weeping ash. 'This is a python tree,' said Anthea. 'Look, you can see the python wound round the trunk.'

'What's a python?' said Robin, backing off.

'Oh, it's just a great big snake that squeezes people to death,' said Anthea. 'A python could easily eat a leopard. That's why leopards won't walk under this tree, you see, Robin.'

Robin looked up. 'Could it eat us?'

'Yes, but it won't if we walk on our heels.' They walked on their heels to the next corner.

'Are there leopards down there?'

'No, but we must never go down there anyway. That's Poison Alley. All the trees are poisonous. They drip poison. If one bit of poison fell on your head, you'd die.'

'I've got my hat on,' said Robin, touching the bobble to make sure.

'It would burn right through your hat,' Anthea assured him. 'Right into your brains. *Fzzzzzzz.*'

They bypassed Poison Alley and walked on over the manhole cover that clanked.

'What's that?'

'That's the Fever Pit. If anyone lifts that manhole cover, they get a terrible disease. There's this terrible disease down there, Robin, and if the lid comes off, the disease will get out and people will die. I should think there's enough disease down there to kill everybody in this town. It's ever so loose, look.'

'Don't lift it! Don't lift it!' Robin screamed, and ran to the shelter for safety.

'Don't go in there,' yelled Anthea. 'That's where the Greasy Witch lives.' Robin bounced out of the shelter as though he were on elastic.

'Where's the Greasy Witch?'

'Oh, you can't see her,' said Anthea, 'but you can tell where she is because she smells so horrible. I think she must be somewhere about. Can't you smell her now?'

Robin sniffed the air and clasped Doggy more tightly.

'And she leaves oily marks wherever she goes. Look, you can see them on the wall.'

Robin looked at the wall. Someone had been very busy, if not the Greasy Witch. Anthea was glad on the whole that Robin could not read.

'The smell's getting worse, isn't it, Robin? I think we'd better go down here and then she won't find us.'

'She'll see us.'

'No, she won't. She can't see with her eyes because they're full of grease. She sees with her ears, but I expect they're all waxy. She's a filthy old witch, really.'

They slipped down a secret-looking path that went round the back of the shelter.

'Is the Greasy Witch down here?' said Robin, fearfully.

'I don't know,' said Anthea. 'Let's investigate.' They tiptoed round the side of the shelter. The path was damp and slippery. 'Filthy old witch. She's certainly *been* here,' said Anthea. 'I think she's gone now. I'll just have a look.'

She craned her neck round the corner of the shelter. There was a sort of glade in the bushes, and in the middle was a stand-pipe, with a tap on top. The pipe was lagged with canvas, like a scaly skin.

'Frightful Corner,' said Anthea. Robin put his cautious head round the edge of the shelter.

'What's that?'

Anthea wondered if it could be a dragon, up on the tip of its tail and ready to strike, but on the other side of the bushes was the brick wall of the King Street Public Conveniences, and at that moment she heard the unmistakable sound of a cistern flushing.

'It's a Lavatory Demon,' she said. 'Quick! We've got to get away before the water stops, or he'll have us.'

They ran all the way to the gates, where they could see the church clock, and it was almost time for lunch.

*

Auntie Lynn fetched Robin home next morning, and three days later she was back again, striding up the path like a warrior queen going into battle, with Robin dangling from her hand, and Doggy dangling from Robin's hand.

Mum took her into the front room, closing the door. Anthea sat on the stairs and listened. Auntie Lynn was in full throat and furious, so it was easy enough to hear what she had to say.

'I want a word with that young lady,' said Auntie Lynn. 'And I want to know what she's been telling him.' Her voice dropped, and Anthea could hear only certain fateful words: 'Leopards . . . poison trees . . . snakes . . . diseases!'

Mum said something very quietly that Anthea did not hear, and then Auntie Lynn turned up the volume once more.

'Won't go to bed unless I leave the door open . . . wants the light on . . . up and down to him all night . . . won't go to the bathroom on his own. He says the – the – ,' she hesitated, 'the *toilet* demons will get him. He nearly broke his neck running downstairs this morning.'

Mum spoke again, but Auntie Lynn cut in like a band-saw.

'Frightened out of his wits! He follows me everywhere.'

The door opened slightly, and Anthea got ready to bolt, but it was Robin who came out, with his thumb in his mouth and circles round his eyes. Under his arm was soggy Doggy, ears chewed to nervous rags.

Robin looked up at Anthea through the bannisters.

'Let's go to the park,' he said.

Sniff Finds a Seagull

Ian Whybrow

I was wondering how you say in French, 'The dog in our kitchen has got hazelnut spread and feathers on.' I could do the first bit all right and I was just thinking to myself that there probably wasn't any French for the rest of it, when I heard Tom's mum scream. This was partly because there *was* a dog in the kitchen with hazelnut spread and feathers on. I was watching him through my periscope, so I should know.

It was a good periscope . . . worked really well. I could see brilliantly into the kitchen from outside on the patio. OK, I could have just looked without using the periscope, but then I could have been seen from indoors. The whole point of a periscope is to look round corners or over things without being seen, so, as I say, this one was dead good. I'd been watching for about five minutes actually. I'd told Mum that I'd keep an eye on my little sister Sal and her friend Tom while she and Tom's mum, Bunty, were upstairs, looking at this wardrobe Mum had just bought at an auction. They were trying to decide whether to strip it or stencil it. I would have chucked it out, but there you are. So I sat at the garden table on the patio and got on with finishing my periscope while Sal and Tom mucked about with a couple of Transformer toys that Tom had brought with him. Sniff had disappeared somewhere.

Sal and Tom enjoyed themselves in their little kiddie way for a bit. They bent the Transformers about and didn't seem to mind if they didn't quite turn into guns or robots. Then they ran up and down on the patio going, 'Do diss!' and 'Look at me!' and then Sal chucked her Transformer at Tom and said, 'I can frow diss!' Tom thought that was a good idea and threw his Transformer as far as he could off the patio on to the lawn. Sal picked hers up and did the same thing. Then they jumped down off the patio and picked up the Transformers and ran back up the two steps and chucked them off again.

The great thing was that while they were whizzing about, they didn't keep coming over to see what I was doing, so I could get on with making the periscope. I'd seen them making one on telly but I reckoned I could improve on it by using masking tape instead of Sellotape and by fitting a little mechanism for altering the angles of the mirrors. I'd had a bit of trouble and several goes at getting the case just right but I cracked the problem just when I thought I was running out of breakfast cereal packets.

I'd just about got it finished when Sal and Tom got fed up with the garden and headed for the kitchen. Handy, because now I could test whether it really worked.

I knelt on the patio, under the window. I could hear cupboard doors being opened and closed. I guessed what was going on and I brought the periscope up to my eye to check my theory. Brilliant! I could see everything ... and there was little Sal dragging a chair up under the cupboard where the jam's kept. She was after the hazelnut spread. The conversation went something like this:

Sal: 'I like some haysnut sped. You like some haysnut sped, Tom?'

Tom: 'Nahh.'

Sal: 'It in nat cupboard.' (Climbs on chair.) 'I get some for you.'

Tom: 'Dome wannenny.'

Sal: 'Here it is. In nis cupboard. Want some? Snice.'

Tom: 'Nahh.'

Sal: (Climbing down with large tub.) 'Can you take da lid off, Tom? I can. Look. Dass easy.'

Tom: 'Wass dat?'

Sal: 'Dass haysnut sped. Dass nice. Here, open you mowff. Nice?'

Tom: '*Pppppppththppp.*'

Sal: 'Don't you like it? Snice.'

At that point, Sal dipped her fingers into the tub, put a handful of the gooey stuff into her own mouth and went '*Pppppppththppp*' because that's what Tom had done. Hazelnut spread spattered over the nearby cupboard doors and on to the floor. Then Tom dipped his fingers into the tub, scooped out some gunge and let Sal have another go. Sal took her turn to scoop some into Tom's mouth. This went on for a bit and then Sniff brought in the dead seagull.

He quite often brings in things if he finds them lying around ... bones, shoes, sticks, old tennis balls, that sort of thing. He brought in a dried cowpat once. He likes smelly things. I think that's why he brought in the seagull. Anyway, as soon as he saw the hazelnut spread, he lost interest in the seagull and dropped it on the kitchen floor. And as soon as Sal and Tom saw the seagull, they lost interest in the hazelnut spread. They changed places and started exploring.

Sniff didn't usually get a proper go at the hazelnut spread and normally had to rely on licking Sal after she'd had some. So he was obviously very interested in the tub and got his head in as far as he could. Likewise, being too noisy and scary to get very close to a real live seagull, Sal and Tom must have thought that *they* were dead lucky to have a chance with this one that Sniff had found, especially as it didn't mind them having a close look at its feathers.

That was how there came to be such a lot of feathers and hazelnut spread on the floor and the cupboard doors and the dog and on Sal and Tom. And it wasn't long after that that Bunty came in and let out a scream that was surprising for a grown-up woman.

'Tommy! Sally! What on earth is going on?' she wailed. 'And oh, good grief! What is THAT?'

'It looks like a seagull,' said Mum. 'And . . . Err!' she clamped her hanky to her nose. 'It smells as if it's been dead for a week.'

Sniff thought he was being congratulated for bringing in something really ace. Wagging the old tail into a fan that wafted a feathery cloud into the air, he darted forward and grabbed the seagull, growling playfully. He jumped up at Mum, planting his sticky great paws on her skirt and his sticky great face in her chest and offering her his prize.

'Get down, Sniff! Sniff, down! No, I don't want that. No!'

'Me have it,' said Sal, stepping forward.

Bunty grabbed her and hauled her up into the air as if she was snatching her from a minefield. Naturally, quite a bit of what had been sticking to Sal transferred to Tom's mum.

Meanwhile, my mum had got the back door open and was pointing outwards towards the distant horizon, calling 'Out! Out!' When that didn't work she got the mop out and half-scooped, half-pushed Sniff into the garden and slammed the door after him.

Sal and Tom squealed furiously. I don't think they were shocked at the treatment Sniff had received from Mum. Actually, they were cheesed off that he'd pinched the seagull they'd been stopped from playing with. Now he was galloping off, down to the field to bury it somewhere near where he'd found it. As I watched him pounding off through the hole in the fence at the bottom of the garden, leaving a few white feathers stuck to the fencing boards on either side of the gap, I wondered what a stranger might think as they saw him galumphing along, fur and feathers waving together in the breeze. Headline: BIRDBEAST CAUSES RIOT ON RECREATION FIELD – TOWNSFOLK FLEE.

'Where's Ben?' said Mum in a voice that got Sal's attention and mine, even though I was outside.

'In da garding.'

'Stupid boy! What's he doing out there? He is supposed to be keeping an eye on you two little terrors! Now look at you. And this place. And me!'

'And me!' added Bunty. 'I am covered in gunk! What *is* this stuff?'

'Haysnut sped,' said Tom, who now knew. 'Snice.'

'And fevvers,' added Sal.

'I don't know about hazelnut – but it certainly does spread,' said Bunty. (Dead witty.) 'It's spread all over this kitchen. How could two little kids make a mess like this in five minutes?'

'Not me and Tom,' said Sal, shaking her head seriously. 'Niff done dat.'

'Nahh,' agreed Tom, who meant 'yeah' but didn't like saying it.

'And I know just the person to clean it all up,' said Mum. 'Ben!'

It was no good me explaining that I *was* keeping an eye on them. Never mind that I didn't take my eye off them. That didn't seem to count. No. I am irresponsible. I am a pain. I have no consideration for others. And I can blinking well clear up the whole sticky, revolting mess. And if I think I'm going out enjoying myself that afternoon, I've got another think coming. All that.

Took me ages to get that place cleaned up. *And* I had to wipe up stuff that wasn't even feathers or hazelnut spread.

It wasn't until Dad came in hours later that anyone showed the least bit of interest in my periscope, either. He thought it was great – and might come in handy for finding things that had rolled under washing machines and sideboards and stuff like that. I think what really finished Mum off was that I'd cut up all the cereal boxes to make the case, so that the raisin bran and the muesli and the Shreddies and the Wheatoes all got mixed up together in the cake tin I tipped them in. That's the trouble with this country, not enough people appreciate the scientific spirit. It could be a genius staring them in the face – and all they can see are a few seagull feathers, a mucked-about muesli and a splash or two of hazelnut spread.

Still, I must say we all had a laugh later on when Sniff came creeping back for his supper and we pounced on him and gave him a bath. But that's another story.

The Pudding Like a Night on the Sea

Ann Cameron

'I'm going to make something special for your mother,' my father said.

My mother was out shopping. My father was in the kitchen looking at the pots and the pans and the jars of this and that.

'What are you going to make?' I said.

'A pudding,' he said.

My father is a big man with wild black hair. When he laughs, the sun laughs in the windowpanes. When he thinks, you can almost see his thoughts sitting on all the tables and chairs. When he is angry, me and my little brother Huey shiver to the bottom of our shoes.

'What kind of pudding will you make?' Huey said.

'A wonderful pudding,' my father said. 'It will taste like a whole raft of lemons. It will taste like a night on the sea.'

Then he took down a knife and sliced five lemons in half. He squeezed the first one. Juice squirted in my eye.

'Stand back!' he said, and squeezed again. The seeds flew out on the floor. 'Pick up those seeds, Huey!' he said.

Huey took the broom and swept them up.

My father cracked some eggs and put the yolks in a pan and the whites in a bowl. He rolled up his sleeves and pushed back his hair and beat up the yolks. 'Sugar, Julian!' he said, and I poured in the sugar.

He went on beating. Then he put in lemon juice and cream and set the pan on the stove. The pudding bubbled and he stirred it fast. Cream splashed on the stove.

'Wipe that up, Huey!' he said.

Huey did.

It was hot by the stove. My father loosened his collar and pushed at his sleeves. The stuff in the pan was getting thicker and thicker. He held the beater up high in the air. 'Just right!' he said, and sniffed in the smell of the pudding.

He whipped the egg whites and mixed them into the pudding. The pudding looked softer and lighter than air.

'Done!' he said. He washed all the pots, splashing water on the floor, and wiped the counter so fast his hair made circles around his head.

'Perfect!' he said. 'Now I'm going to take a nap. If something important happens, bother me. If nothing important happens, don't bother me. And – the pudding is for your mother. Leave the pudding alone!'

He went to the living room and was asleep in a minute, sitting straight up in his chair.

Huey and I guarded the pudding.

'Oh, it's a wonderful pudding,' Huey said.

'With waves on the top like the ocean,' I said.

'I wonder how it tastes,' Huey said.

'Leave the pudding alone,' I said.

46

'If I just put my finger in there I'll know how it tastes,' Huey said.

And he did it.

'You did it!' I said. 'How does it taste?'

'It tastes like a whole raft of lemons,' he said. 'It tastes like a night on the sea.'

'You've made a hole in the pudding!' I said. 'But since you did it, I'll have a taste.' And it tasted like a whole night of lemons. It tasted like floating at sea.

'It's such a big pudding,' Huey said. 'It can't hurt to have a little more.'

'Since you took more, I'll have more,' I said.

'That was a bigger lick than I took!' Huey said. 'I'm going to have more again.'

'Whoops!' I said.

'You put in your whole hand!' Huey said. 'Look at the pudding you spilled on the floor!'

'I am going to clean it up,' I said. And I took the rag from the sink.

'That's not really clean,' Huey said.

'It's the best I can do,' I said.

'Look at the pudding!' Huey said.

It looked like craters on the moon. 'We have to smooth this over,' I said. 'So it looks the way it did before! Let's get spoons.'

And we evened the top of the pudding with spoons, and while we evened it, we ate some more.

'There isn't much left,' I said.

'We were supposed to leave the pudding alone.' Huey said.

'We'd better get away from here,' I said. We ran into our bedroom and crawled under the bed. After a long time we heard my father's voice.

'Come into the kitchen, dear,' he said. 'I have something for you.'

'Why, what is it?' my mother said, out in the kitchen.

Under the bed, Huey and I pressed ourselves to the wall.

'Look,' said my father, out in the kitchen. 'A wonderful pudding.'

'Where is the pudding?' my mother said.

'WHERE ARE YOU, BOYS?' my father said. His voice went through every crack and corner of the house.

We felt like two leaves in a storm.

'WHERE ARE YOU? I SAID!' My father's voice was booming.

Huey whispered to me, 'I'm scared.'

We heard my father walking slowly through the rooms.

'Huey!' he called. 'Julian!'

We could see his feet. He was coming into our room.

He lifted the bedspread. There was his face, and his eyes like black lightning. He grabbed us by the legs and pulled. 'STAND UP!' he said.

We stood.

'What do you have to tell me?' he said.

'We went outside,' Huey said, 'and when we came back, the pudding was gone!'

'Then why were you hiding under the bed?' my father said.

We didn't say anything. We looked at the floor.

'I can tell you one thing,' he said. 'There is going to be some beating here now! There is going to be some whipping!'

The curtains at the window were shaking. Huey was holding my hand.

'Go into the kitchen! my father said. 'Right now!'

We went into the kitchen.

'Come here, Huey!' my father said.

Huey walked towards him, his hands behind his back.

'See these eggs?' my father said. He cracked them and put the yolks in a pan and set the pan on the counter. He stood a chair by the counter. 'Stand up here,' he said to Huey.

Huey stood on the chair by the counter.

'Now it's time for your beating!' my father said.

Huey started to cry. His tears fell in with the egg yolks.

'Take this!' my father said. My father handed him the egg beater. 'Now beat those eggs,' he said. 'I want this to be a good beating!'

'Oh!' Huey said. He stopped crying. And he beat the egg yolks.

'Now you, Julian, stand here!' my father said.

I stood on a chair by the table.

'I hope you're ready for your whipping!'

I didn't answer. I was afraid to say yes or no.

'Here!' he said, and he set the egg whites in front of me. 'I want these whipped and whipped well!'

'Yes, sir!' I said, and started whipping.

My father watched us. My mother came into the kitchen and watched us.

After a while Huey said, 'This is hard work.'

'That's too bad,' my father said. 'Your beating's not done!' And he added sugar and cream and lemon juice to Huey's pan and put the pan on the stove. And Huey went on beating.

'My arm hurts from whipping,' I said.

'That's too bad,' my father said. 'Your whipping's not done.'

So I whipped and whipped, and Huey beat and beat.

'Hold that beater in the air, Huey!' my father said.

Huey held it in the air.

'See!' my father said. 'A good pudding stays on the beater. It's thick enough now. Your beating's done.' Then he turned to me. 'Let's see those egg whites, Julian!' he said. They were puffed up and fluffy. 'Congratulations, Julian!' he said. 'Your whipping's done.'

He mixed the egg whites into the pudding himself. Then he passed the pudding to my mother.

'A wonderful pudding,' she said. 'Would you like some, boys?'

'No thank you,' we said.

She picked up a spoon. 'Why, this tastes like a whole raft of lemons,' she said. 'This tastes like a night on the sea.'

Sisterlist

Rowena Sommerville

My big sister says she loves me,
says she'll take me round the town,
Mum says, 'Ooh, you are a brick,
you never let your old ma down.
Now I won't be long, I promise,
get yourselves some chips to eat',
gives my sister something extra,
'that's 'cos you deserve a treat,
and I know that I can trust you,
be good girls and please don't fight';
as she closed the door, my sister
pointed at me and said,
                                    'RIGHT –
don't imagine that I like you,
I'm just giving Mum a hand,
I can't go if I don't take you,
and I need the money and
don't you walk too close behind me,
don't wear knee-socks or a hat,
please don't pose or pick your nose,

and don't you look at me like that,
don't ask me to go in toyshops,
you can see I'm much too hip,
don't wear clothes that look as though
they came from Oxfam's lucky dip,

if we see some tasty lads
then please attempt some sort of cool,
and don't embarrass me by smirking
if we meet some kids from school,
and don't go touching things in Woolworths,
don't you wear that gruesome coat,
and when I'm chatting with my friends
don't cough, or hum, or clear your throat,
and don't start whingeing that you're bored,

or moaning that you've had enough,
and don't tell me you've got a blister,
learn to bear it, life is tough,
don't go pulling funny faces,
don't go asking me for dosh,
and if you're spoken to, act normal,
don't talk common, don't talk posh,

and don't butt in on conversations,
don't ear-hole the things we say,
if some nice boy chats me up,
then have the sense to walk away,
don't go asking me for ice cream,
DON'T act like a little kid,
don't go telling tales at home,
and don't blame me for what YOU did,
and don't tell Mum I'm wearing lipstick,
no-one likes a dirty sneak,
and if you give me any grief
I'll beat you up at school next week.'

Well, all of this went on for ages,
then we heard the back door key,
Mum came in, said, 'Back so soon, girls?
Who'll make me a cup of tea?
Are you two behaving well?
Was that a quarrel that I heard?'
and then I looked at my big sister,
but I didn't say a word.

My Gran's Jumper

Kathryn Cave

My gran knitted me a jumper.

I tried it on. 'Thanks, Gran,' I said. 'I'll wear it to school next year.'

'He's joking, Mum,' said my mother. She gave me a look. 'He'll wear it to school tomorrow morning, that's what he'll do.'

My sister Deb came up behind and poked me in the back. She's always doing that, as if I don't know how to behave.

''Course I'll wear it, Gran,' I said. 'I can't stand a jumper that's too tight. Thank you very much for making it.' I gave her a hug and then it was time to go home.

In the car I said, 'If I'm wearing that jumper tomorrow, could you boil it up or something this evening, Mum, so it'll shrink a bit?' Because, honestly, it wasn't small.

'Don't be ungrateful, Sean,' said my mother. 'Think how long it must have taken your gran to knit that, all the balls of wool it must have used.

The least you can do is wear it.'

'I will wear it,' I said. 'I never said I wouldn't wear it. I need a bit of time, that's all. I'm not going to grow that much overnight.' If you want to know the truth, you could have put our whole school football team inside that jumper, reserves and all, and still have had space left over to rent out. It wasn't so much a jumper as a tent.

'Gran must think you're Goliath,' said Deb. 'Or a gorilla. The length of those arms . . .'

'That's enough,' my mother said. 'I don't want to hear any more about it.'

That night when I went to bed she put out the jumper on my chair, along with the clothes I always wear to school. I tried being tactful.

'It's not that I don't like it, Mum. It isn't really. Only I've got football practice at lunch and I can't play football wearing that.'

'Why ever not?'

'Come on, Mum. Be reasonable. It'd be like playing football in a dress.'

'Take it off first then,' was all she said.

'I won't have time.' I told her all about Monday lunch-time, how it was my turn to clean out the gerbils and then I had to program the computer for the infants to play Pac Man. I wasn't going to have time to breathe before football practice, let alone change out of Gran's jumper. You don't get in and out of something like that in a hurry.

It was no good.

'You're wearing that jumper tomorrow and that's that,' said my mother, slamming down a pair of socks on top of the pile of clothes. 'Your room's a mess. Tidy it up as soon as you get back from school tomorrow or there'll be trouble.'

Next morning I got up and put on my clothes, all except the jumper. I took it down with me to the kitchen where the rest were having breakfast. I had one last hope.

'I don't really have to wear this, do I, Dad?' I held up the jumper so he could see it in all its glory.

'If your mother says so,' he said.

'I do say so,' said my mother. 'Put it on and eat your breakfast.'

That was that. I put the jumper on.

Deb started spluttering into her cornflakes. 'Where've his hands got to?' I was wondering the same myself, as a matter of fact.

'It'll be perfectly all right,' my mother said, rolling up my sleeves about a metre. 'There, you see!' You couldn't, actually – not my hands, anyway. Even rolled up the sleeves came down to the tips of my fingers.

'Yes,' said my father. 'It isn't bad at all. You'd never guess he had holes in the knees of his trousers.'

'You'd never guess he had trousers at all,' said

Deb. 'It's a shame it's so short, though. A few more rows and he wouldn't have needed shoes either. Just think of the money saved.' She went off to catch the bus, whistling.

I wasn't quite so happy. Mum watched me from the gate all the way to the end of our road. I couldn't take the jumper off until I was round the corner. Then I bundled it up as small as it would go and put it in my bag. It felt wonderful to be free again. My bag, though – how could Gran have knitted something so heavy? She must have had to use specially reinforced steel needles. By the time I got to school both my arms were aching.

In the classroom I had to take out the jumper to get at my books and the stuff I needed in class.

'Hurry up, Sean!' said Miss Harvey, our teacher. 'Don't forget you're down to teach Mrs Browning in Infants Three about Space Invaders before assembly. And later on I want you to give me a hand with the newts. What's that you've got there?'

I was still trying to bundle up the jumper. It seemed to have got bigger. It was an awful struggle to get it back into the bag. Whatever happened I wasn't going to tell Miss Harvey it was a jumper. She might have told me to wear it.

'It's a sort of knitted blanket,' I said. She gave me a funny look, but I stuffed the jumper back inside the bag at last and went to turn on the computer for Mrs Browning.

After that the morning went just as normal, right up to after lunch. I had just finished my fourth and last peanut butter and jam sandwich when Paul came up.

'What about the gerbils?' he asked. There was about ten minutes to go before football practice because Mr Bunyan the coach is a slow eater, so we went back into the classroom and got busy.

The gerbils live in a big old cage on top of *Oxford Junior English* and *New Worlds to Conquer*. There are two of them: Grumpy and Dopey. They have a pretty boring life, up there on top of the bookshelves. They can't even look out of the window because the cage is the wrong way round. Dopey does nothing but sleep and eat. Grumpy sometimes chews a bit of stick or gnaws at the wire at the front of the cage. He has also been known to gnaw at other things, including fingers.

Paul and I had done this job hundreds of times before so we had it pretty well organized. We put both the gerbils in the waste-paper basket while we cleared the old straw out of their cage and put in some fresh. Then I refilled the water bottle and Paul gave them a clean bowl of nuts and seeds.

Then, because there was still four minutes left before football practice, I let Dopey run about for a bit on top of my table while Paul took Grumpy on a grand tour of the classroom. This was to make up to them for having such a dull time in general. We were all having a good time – then, disaster. Grumpy isn't called Grumpy for nothing. Right in the middle of the tour, while Paul was introducing him to the newts, Grumpy bit Paul on the finger and Paul dropped him.

This was a real emergency. I had to put Dopey somewhere safe while I helped Paul catch Grumpy. My bag was under the table, so I unzipped it, put Dopey in on top of my jumper, and zipped it up again.

Well, we got Grumpy out of the newt tank in the end and dried him off on my football shirt. He wasn't at all grateful, and he bit me too as I was putting him back in the cage. Then the whistle blew so Paul and I had to dash and put our boots on for the practice.

It is not true that I forgot about Dopey. I remembered him right in the middle of the last lesson that afternoon, but I couldn't do anything about him then. I knew he'd be all right in the bag until going home time. I could hear him squeaking and scrabbling. As soon as Miss Harvey went out of the classroom to talk to someone, I whipped Dopey out of my bag and popped him back in the cage. Then I went home.

The first thing my mother said when I took off my coat was: 'Where's your new jumper?'

'Yes,' said Deb, who was eating toast and honey. 'The holes in your knees are showing.'

'It was too hot. I had to take it off,' I said.

'I hope you haven't got it all creased. Get it out and I'll see if it needs an iron,' said my mother.

I got it out. 'Look,' I said. 'It's perfectly okay,

Mum.' And I held it up. It felt different somehow.
Lighter.

Then I saw. It wasn't like a tent any more. It was
like a mosquito net. Full of holes. Hundreds of
them.

Even Deb stopped chewing for a minute. 'Moths?' she asked my mother, who was speechless.

'No, not moths,' I told them sadly. 'Gerbils. One little gerbil.' Dopey had certainly had a busy afternoon.

When my mother got her voice back she said a lot of things. 'And don't you ever expect your poor grandmother to knit anything for you again,' she finished, 'if you can't take better care of your clothes than that.'

'No,' I said. 'I see that. I'm sorry, Mum.'

Deb was scraping the last of the honey out of the pot and I hadn't had any tea at all. The way things were I wasn't going to get any for a long time either. There was my room to clear up, then vacuuming the hall, then cleaning out the bathroom, and all the other special jobs my mother keeps to use in emergencies like this.

At the kitchen door a thought struck me. Maybe every cloud does have a silver lining. 'Next time, Mum,' I said, 'maybe Gran could knit something for Deb instead?'

And I went upstairs to tidy my room.

My Dad

Anne Fine

I knew Dad worked in a big garage about a hundred and fifty miles down the motorway, but whenever I asked Mum anything more about him, she only said:

'Oh, he's all right.'

It isn't much to build on, is it?

'Well, is he *good looking*?'

'He looks all right.'

'Is he *intelligent*?'

'His brain works all right.'

'Is he *amusing*?'

'He made me laugh all right, I suppose.'

'Is he *kind*?'

'He was always all right with me and the cats.'

I lost my temper then.

'If he was never any better than *all right*,' I snapped, 'why did you bother to have *me*?'

Mum laughed, and stretched out her hand to stroke my hair.

'Oh, *you*,' she said. 'You're all right, too, you are.'

You see? Hopeless. Absolutely hopeless. So I gave up.

But then, a few days later in school, we started something new: a project on Families. Mr Russell told everyone to be quiet, and then he tossed up to see whether we were to start with mothers or fathers. And fathers won, so fathers it was.

'I haven't got one,' Andrew said.

'Neither have I.'

'Mine's in Australia.'

'Lucky you!'

Then Mr Russell told everyone to be quiet again.

'If you haven't got your own, real, original, biological father,' he said, 'pick out the person who comes closest. Pick someone – ' He paused, and waved his hands around in the air, searching for an example. 'Pick someone you would ask to fix your bike.'

'I haven't got a bike,' said Joel.

'My mum always fixes my bike,' said Sarah.

'I *asked* my dad to fix my bike,' grumbled Arif. 'Six weeks ago! He hasn't even *looked* at it yet.' He scowled, and added with real bitterness: '*And* he's my own, real, original, biological dad.'

'My uncle fixes my bike. He's got a bike shop.'

'Nothing has ever gone wrong with my bike.'

'I've never even had a bike,' Joel said sadly.

'At least you've got a father,' said Andrew.

Joel was just telling us he thought he'd much

prefer a bike, when Mr Russell told everyone to be quiet again.

'Father,' he said. 'Or someone like it. I want a picture or a photograph, and two whole sides of writing, by Friday.'

We all groaned loudly. And by the time Mr Russell had told everyone to be quiet again, the bell had rung.

I ran off home.

Mum was leaning against the draining-board. She was wearing her plum-coloured plastic boots and her fishnet stockings. She was fiddling with her tarantula earrings. Crusher Maggot, my mum's boyfriend, was slouching at the kitchen table, wearing funny dark glasses and playing a tune on his skull with his knuckles.

What do they *do* all day long when I'm away at school, that's what I'd like to know.

I asked Mum: 'Do you have a photo of my real dad?'

'Yes,' she said. 'No. I don't know. No. Yes.'

I do try to be very patient.

'Which?' I said. 'Yes or no?'

'Both, really,' she replied. 'I do have a photo of him, yes. But I'm afraid that my left elbow got in front of most of his face, and what little of him is showing is terribly blurry. You'd never know that it was him.'

'Weren't there any other photos?'

Mum tipped her head on one side to think. One of the tarantula earrings crawled over her cheek, and the other got tangled in her hair. It was very off-putting.

'There were some others,' she recalled. 'But you were in them, too, so he took those with him.'

I thought that was a little daft, myself. One of them might have realized I would grow up, and want to see them. But, still as patient as could be, I asked: 'Where is this famous photo of part of his blurred face and your left elbow?'

'I'm not sure,' Mum said. 'I think I've lost it.'

(I simply can't *think* why they call it 'home' work. I'd stand a better chance of getting it done on the *moon*.)

'I need a photo,' I told her, 'to take to school.'

'Take that nice one of Crusher,' she told me.

I've mentioned this photograph of Crusher before, I think. Do you remember? It's the one with his hair in flaming red and orange spikes, and his teeth ferociously bared, and his tattoo showing.

'No, thank you,' I answered as politely as possible. 'I'd like one of my own, real, original, biological father.'

'All right,' said Crusher. 'Suit yourself. I'll ask him for one next time I see him.'

I turned and stared.

'*See* him?' I said. 'Do you get to see him?'

'Quite often,' Crusher said. 'I always fill up with petrol at his garage. Why, I stopped in and had a couple of words with him only a week ago.'

I was amazed. Simply amazed.

'How is he?' I asked. 'How is my very own, real, original, biological father?'

Crusher wasn't at all irritated by this display of crippling sarcasm.

'All right,' he said. 'He was all right.'

But Mum was a little put out by my rudeness.

'Original and biological he may be,' she said. 'But who fixes your bike?'

(I'd really like to know where they pick up all this fix-your-bike business.)

I was still angry.

'Next time,' I said, as cold as ice, 'next time that

someone drops in to have a few words with my own, real, original, biological father, do you think they might possibly bother to mention it to me?'

'I'll do better than that,' Crusher offered. 'I'll take you down there.'

'When?'

'When you like.'

I thought about it.

'I need the photo before Friday,' I told him.

'Tomorrow, then.'

'*All right*,' I said. 'Tomorrow. *All right*.'

So that's how it came about that the very next day I borrowed next door's fancy new camera, and Crusher borrowed the other side's car since his own still wasn't going, and I travelled with him all the way down the motorway. It meant I had to take the whole afternoon off school. Mum said it didn't matter since I'd be doing school work in taking the photo; but I didn't dare tell that one to Mr Russell. That sort of thinking really annoys him. He calls it 'slack'. I did consider trying to explain, but he was in one of his terribly busy moods and in the end I just did what everyone else in the class does, and told him that I had to go to the dentist.

It took Crusher and me exactly two hours and forty minutes to drive down the motorway as far as the garage.

It was a big one, set back a little from the road. There were several lines of pumps, and every one of them was busy with people filling cars and motorbikes.

Crusher pulled up beside the air and water.

'Tell you what,' he suggested, picking next door's fancy new camera off the back seat and thrusting it into my hands. 'I'll give you over to your own, real, original, biological dad, and then I'll nip off for a while and do what I was going to do.'

'What *were* you going to do?' I asked, suddenly suspicious.

First Crusher looked blank, then a little bit shifty.

'I really haven't the time to stop and explain,' he told me.

I gave him a look – one of my *searching* looks.

'You drove all the way down here just to bring me to see my dad, didn't you?' I accused him.

'No, I didn't,' said Crusher.

'Oh yes you did.'

'No, I didn't.'

'You did. I can tell.'

'All right,' said Crusher, embarrassed. '*All right.* Maybe I did, but I certainly didn't drive all this way just to sit in the front seat of the car arguing with you.'

And he got out.

I followed. Crusher was looking round the garage forecourt. Suddenly he nudged my elbow.

'There,' he said, nodding towards a man in overalls who was bending over a pile of cut-price tyres.

'There he is.'

'Really?'

'Yes. That's him.'

And Crusher bellowed across the crowded forecourt:

'Hey, Bill! *Bill*! Here's your young Minna come to see you!'

The man in overalls lifted his head and stared in our direction. I say 'our' direction, but it was only 'my' direction by then, because Crusher Maggot had disappeared in a flash after making his announcement, and I was left standing alone on the petrol-station forecourt, clutching a camera, and ten yards from my own, real, original, biological father I hadn't seen for ages.

It was all right. In fact, he was jolly nice, really. He gave me tons of comics and free bars of chocolate from the garage shop, and a brand-new film for the people next door to make up for my borrowing their camera. He helped me take a lot of photos, and even showed me how to set the time-release button so we could get some of us standing together with his arm round my shoulders. He made me promise to send him copies of all the ones that came out properly, and he laughed like a drain when I told him about the only photo of him that Mum has left.

He asked quite a lot of questions about our family, and he seemed pretty interested when I told him all about Crummy Dummy, my baby sister. He said he was glad to hear I had company now, and he made me promise to send a photo of her, too. And a good one of Mum.

He asked me about school, and my friends, and the house. He said that he was very pleased to hear I could swim, and he sounded interested in my roller-skating. Then he left someone else looking after the forecourt, and took me for a spin up the motorway in one of the open sports cars parked round the back of the garage.

That was fantastic. The wind blew my hair till it stuck out like Mum's. (He said I looked a bit like Mum, anyway.) He drove miles faster than Crusher Maggot does, and when I told him so, he grinned, and said that he was glad to hear it.

I didn't know quite what to call him. I tried to say the word 'Dad' once or twice, but it sort of got stuck because I didn't know him well enough yet. Then he said: 'Why don't you just call me Bill? Everyone else does.' And that was easier.

When we drove back towards the garage, I could see Crusher standing, waiting, on the forecourt.

Bill slowed the car right down. And just before we came close enough for Crusher to overhear, he asked me privately: 'Do you get on with him? Is he all right?'

I looked at Crusher, who was watching me anxiously to see how I was getting on with my own, real, original, biological father.

'Yes,' I said. 'He's all right.'

'Good,' Bill said. 'Good.'

So that was that, really. The three of us shared a quick cup of tea out of the machine, and I ate one more chocolate bar, and took one more for the journey. Bill insisted on filling the car up for nothing. 'It's not every day my daughter comes down to visit me,' he said. Then Crusher and I got in and drove off.

I waved, and Bill waved and shouted that he'd

pop in next time he came up our way, and I was to give his best wishes to Mum. Then we were out of sight.

Crusher settled himself more comfortably in the seat, then: 'Well?'

'All right,' I told him. 'He was all right.'

When we got home, it was dark. Mum was really pleased to see us. All of the photos came out fine. Some were really good. (I've got the best ones pinned on my bedroom wall now.) I even managed the two whole pages of writing about my own, real, original, biological father – though I could tell that Mr Russell was really disappointed that I'd chosen to do him instead of Crusher Maggot, whom he's seen hanging around for me at the school gates.

And now, as you can see, I'm in the habit too. Yesterday, when Arif and I were sitting on the curbside watching poor Crusher trying to fix our bikes, Arif asked me what my real father was like. And, without even thinking, I answered: 'Oh, he's all right.'

Sometimes I worry that I'm getting just like all the rest of them, honestly I do.

Computer Games

Gene Kemp

'Let me have a go, Tony,' said my kid brother Adam.

I scowled at him. 'No, I'm playing it. Push off.'

'You've been playing it for ages. I wanna go.'

'No, you don't. I'm older than you and what I say goes. It's my computer. Go and watch telly.'

'It's not yours. It was a present to both of us. We're supposed to share it.'

I began to feel ratty. Dear brother Adam always got on my wick.

The pair of us were stuck in on a wet, gloomy Saturday afternoon so I'd gone up to my room to play on the computer, telling everybody that I was doing my homework. After all since I couldn't go out and there wasn't much on TV, why not? Unfortunately, I shared the bedroom with my younger brother Adam who pestered me.

'You're no good at playing it. Your go never lasts longer than a minute. You're rubbish. A waste of time,' I said.

'I can beat you. Try me on two players. I bet you're scared to play me.'

'I can't be bothered to play against you. I could beat you with my eyes shut. Do something else, go someplace else. Anywhere. Just leave me alone.'

'It's my room too. I can stay if I want.'

'Well, shut your face. I can't concentrate with you rabbiting on,' I snarled.

'Are you going to let me have a go, then?'

'I'll let you have a punch in the head if you don't shut up. You're messing my game up.'

'You rotten pig. I'll tell Mum on you.'

'You die if you do. Now get out.'

'No, I won't.'

I got off my chair and advanced on him. He fled quickly. After all he's only eight and I'm eleven so I'm The Boss.

I shut the door and returned to the computer. It felt nice and quiet on my own again. I got into playing my Space Invaders game. I wanted to beat my best high score. All around lay scattered the games I'd been playing that afternoon: computer football, golf, tennis, motor racing, flying, snooker, olympics etc. But my favourites were the Space games, the most difficult, the most challenging of *all.*

I found the Space Diamonds disc and inserted it into the machine. The object of this game was to collect diamonds and shoot various space aliens with a spaceship. It was fast, it was exciting with its different levels and passwords.

I played non-stop until Mum yelled 'Tea-time!' from the bottom of the stairs. I had to finish my go, then I heard her yell again. So I went downstairs. Reluctantly.

I sat down beside my brother, opposite Mum and Dad.

'You've been quiet today, Tony,' said Dad. 'Working hard?'

'Yes, I've got a lot of stuff to catch up with,' I replied. They didn't like me playing the computer for long, saying it was bad for me. Adam muttered under his breath so I kicked him under the table.

'Tony, can you play with Adam this evening?' asked Mum. 'He's all bored and miserable today.'

'I would do if I wasn't so busy,' I said. 'I've got this essay to finish for English.'

'Why don't you play on the computer, Adam?' said Dad. 'After all, Tony isn't using it if he's doing his homework, is he?'

He gave me an amused look as if he didn't believe me. I stared at Adam hard.

'I only like playing it with Tony,' he said finally.

'Well, when Tony's finished his work, I expect he'll play with you,' said Mum.

Tea finished at last, thank Heaven. I left the table quickly, anxious to get back to the game.

'Anybody going to help me with the dishes and

clearing up?' asked Mum.

'Adam will. After all, he's got nothing else to do.' I grinned at him and he glared back.

Having volunteered Adam for washing up, I quickly returned to the computer and resettled myself.

Soon a familiar face peered round the door.

'Can I have a go now, Tony?'

'No, you can't. You're no good at it. You can watch if you want, as long as you shut up.'

'I don't want to watch you play. It's boring. You take it seriously. It's only a bit of fun.'

'Well, buzz off then. Go and watch telly or something, just leave me alone.'

'I've got a new game I want to play. I'll show you.'

'I don't want to know. Get lost. Your games are boring.'

'I hate you, you big-head. You think you're so great. Drop dead,' he bawled.

'If you haven't gone in three seconds you've had it,' I said.

He didn't move. I started to get up.

'Don't say I didn't warn you.' I moved in on him.

He fled at speed. I grinned as I sat down again. He'd be too scared to say anything.

I made myself comfortable and started playing Space Diamonds again. I was playing well today and felt that I could beat my high score and get on to higher levels.

I began to feel more and more excited as I progressed further than I had ever done before. I went from the first level, which was fairly easy, to the second, third and fourth levels, each of which was harder than the previous one. Soon I got to level five, which I'd never got past before, as you had to get through a minefield which was very tough.

I stayed at this level for ages, determined this time to get through it. It frustrated me and I longed to see what came next.

Eventually I made it through the minefield and slumped in the chair sweating. My heart and pulse beat like mad. Now to see what came next. I might even be able to complete the whole game.

The sixth level was a fast, frantic affair but less tricky than the previous one, and before long I had completed this one too.

I felt great. After trying for ages I had now got two levels further.

However, the seventh level was extremely hard, a narrow maze to get through, almost impossible without crashing the ship.

I played on and on, determined to get through the maze, sure that I could do it sooner or later. I became totally absorbed by the game and started to play it automatically. I lost any feeling in my eyes and fingers and there was no time. The screen blurred. It changed, though in my hypnotized state I couldn't really see clearly as a new game appeared, one I hadn't played before.

I was a small figure on the ground with trees and rocks and a spaceship on the other side of the screen. Evil aliens, all in shifting, varying colours appeared in the sky and fired lightning bolts at me. I swerved to dodge them, all that practice coming in useful, fired my ray gun back at them and headed for the ship. One of the aliens fired a bolt into the figure on the screen and pain shot into my arm, as if it was me in the screen. And it was. I was hot and throbbing and the game was for real. I dodged behind the rocks and trees and fired frantically as I headed for the spaceship, heart pounding like mad. I made it by the skin of my teeth.

Then the ship took off, heading for the aliens in the sky. I shot hundreds of them, but as quickly as I did this hundreds more appeared. Enemy spaceships surrounded me as I zoomed onwards into the sky. I operated a force field to deflect the scores of missiles aimed at me.

This was a computer game I wasn't enjoying at all. I'd gone over the top and I was scared to death.

After a while the alien ships fell back and I saw a large planet appearing on the screen. It looked grey and desolate and frightening. My ship slowed down as I approached.

I didn't want to land. I wanted to stop but I couldn't. My head ached and I felt sick and tired.

A gap appeared in the side of the planet now filling the screen. I shot down this narrow tunnel not much wider than the ship and it almost scraped the sides as I sped along. Twice I almost crashed and then to my horror dragons appeared in the corridor breathing fire at the ship and monsters flung themselves against it. Each time the ship was jolted it went right through me as well. I could hear the bloodcurdling shrieks and squeals of the monsters as I shot them.

Then the corridor widened into a large cave. Somehow I knew we'd reached the centre of the planet. Inside it loomed a horrible skeleton-like figure wearing a cape and holding a sickle in its bony hands. It was all I'd ever wanted in a computer game and all I didn't want NOW.

It grew larger and larger as I was drawn nearer it. I fired all of my weapons with no effect. Its empty eye sockets and rictus teeth grinned at me. Its sickle swung against the side of the ship, slashing it open. I was flung out.

The face now filled the screen. Skeletal arms grabbed me and pulled me struggling towards the mouth. Oh, the pain! I was being eaten alive. My bones were being crushed.

I woke up, gasping, my head on fire. The room

was dark. Somehow I turned on the light.

'What are you doing now?' my brother groaned irritably from his bed. 'First you fall asleep by the computer and now you make funny noises all night. What's wrong with you?'

'Oh, shut up, I said, starting to recover. 'I was just having a nightmare.'

'Good,' said Adam and went back to sleep. And so did I.

I awoke late in the morning feeling terrible. My brother was already up and having a game on the computer. I wandered groggily over to him.

'What's that you're playing?' I asked, looking at the screen.

'My new game. It's great. I suppose you want to play now.'

'No, I don't. What's it called?'

'Planet Skull. It's the best game I ever played.'

And the figure appeared on the screen, the one from my dream last night. It grinned knowingly at me.

'Sure you don't want to play?' asked Adam.

I ran out of that room quickly.

'Good. Now I've got it all to myself,' Adam said and turned back to the game grinning.

The Runaway Reptiles

Margaret Mahy

Sir Hamish Hawthorn, the famous old explorer, was not happy.

'Oh, Marilyn,' he cried to his favourite niece. 'I long to go exploring up the Orinoco river once more, but who will look after my pets?'

'The Reverend Crabtree next door will feed the cats, I'm sure,' said Marilyn. 'He is a very kind-hearted man. And I will take care of the alligator for you.'

'But Marilyn,' Sir Hamish said, 'what about your neighbour? He might object to alligators.'

Marilyn lived in Marigold Avenue – a most respectable street. The house next door was exactly the same as hers. It had the same green front door, the same garden and the same marigolds. A man called Archie Lightfoot lived there. He was rather handsome, but being handsome was not everything. Would he enjoy having a twenty-foot Orinoco alligator next door?

'Don't worry, Uncle dear,' said Marilyn. 'I shall work something out.'

At that exact moment, by a curious coincidence, Archie Lightfoot was opening an important-looking letter.

Dear Mr Lightfoot, he read.
Your great-aunt – who died last week – has left you her stamp album, full of rare and valuable stamps.

'Terrific!' shouted Archie. Though he had never met his great-aunt, he had inherited her great love of stamps. Now, it seemed, he had inherited her stamp album as well. He read on eagerly.

There is one condition. You must give a good home to your aunt's twenty-foot Nile crocodile. If you refuse, you don't get the stamp collection. Those are the terms of the will.

'What will Marilyn Hawthorn say?' muttered Archie Lightfoot. 'A beautiful girl like that will not want a twenty-foot Nile crocodile on the lawn next door. I will have to work something out.'

That night, Marilyn Hawthorn tossed and turned. She could not sleep. In the end she decided to get up and make herself some toast. She could see the light next door shining on the marigolds. Archie Lightfoot was evidently having something to eat as well.

There is something about midnight meals that makes people have clever ideas. Sure enough, on the stroke of twelve, Marilyn Hawthorn suddenly

thought of the answer to her problem.

The next day she ran up a large blue sun bonnet and a pretty shawl on her sewing machine, and borrowed the biggest motorized wheelchair she could find. Then she went round to her uncle's house.

Before leaving for the Orinoco, Uncle Hamish helped his niece settle the alligator comfortably in the wheelchair, packing it in with lots of wet cushions. The big sun bonnet nearly hid its snout, but Marilyn made it wear sunglasses to help the disguise.

'I shan't forget this,' Sir Hamish said in a deeply grateful voice.

'Neither shall I,' murmured Marilyn, wheeling the alligator out into the street.

As Marilyn pushed the disguised alligator through her front gate she noticed Archie Lightfoot pushing a large motorized wheelchair through his front gate, too. Sitting in it was someone muffled in a scarf, a floppy hat and sunglasses.

'My old grandfather is coming to live with me for a while,' Archie said with a nervous laugh.

'How funny!' said Marilyn. 'My old granny is coming to stay with *me*.'

The two old grandparents looked at each other through their sunglasses and grinned toothily.

'Unfortunately,' Archie added quickly, 'my old grandfather can sometimes be very crabby. He has a big heart, but occasionally he works himself up into a bad temper. Do warn your grandmother not to talk to him.'

'I have the same problem with Granny,' Marilyn replied. 'She is basically big hearted, but at times she can be bad tempered. If you try to talk to her when she's hungry, she just snaps your head off!'

At first, things went smoothly. Every day Marilyn gave the alligator a large breakfast of fish and tomato sauce. Then she tucked the huge reptile into the wheelchair with blankets soaked in home-made mud. Next, she wheeled it into the garden and settled it down with a bottle of cordial, an open tin of sardines and the newspaper. The alligator always looked eagerly over the fence to see what was going on next door.

In his garden, Archie Lightfoot was settling his old grandfather down with tuna fish sandwiches and a motoring magazine. His grandfather blew a daring kiss to Marilyn Hawthorn's grandmother. Marilyn saw her alligator blow one back.

'You are not to blow kisses to a respectable old gentleman,' she said sternly. The grandfather blew another kiss and the alligator did the same. Marilyn smacked its paw. It tried to bite her, but she was much too quick for it.

While Marilyn Hawthorn and Archie Lightfoot were at work, the two old grandparents blew kisses to one another and tossed fishy snacks across the fence.

That evening, when Marilyn Hawthorn got home, she noticed that her alligator seemed rather ill. It sighed a great deal, and merely toyed with its sardines at supper. Marilyn felt its forehead. It was warm and feverish, a bad thing in alligators, which are, of course, cold-blooded. She took it to the vet at once.

'What on earth is this?' cried the vet, listening to the alligator's heart. 'This alligator is in love!'

The alligator sighed so deeply it accidentally swallowed the vet's thermometer.

'It must be homesick for the Orinoco,' Marilyn thought to herself. So she took a day off work, wrapped cool mudpacks around the alligator, and put it in the marigold garden – with a large photograph of the Orinoco river to look at.

As she was doing this, Archie Lightfoot's face appeared over the garden fence.

'Oh, I'm so worried about my grandfather,' he cried. 'I have had to take him to the vet – I mean, the doctor – and he sighed so deeply that he swallowed a stethoscope.'

'And I've had to take the day off work to look after my old granny,' said Marilyn. '*She* has swallowed a thermometer.'

'Ahem!' coughed Archie Lightfoot, clearing his throat nervously. 'Perhaps, since you are taking the day off work, you might like to slip over and see my stamp collection.'

'I'd love to,' replied Marilyn.

Marilyn Hawthorn and Archie Lightfoot spent rather a long time looking at the stamp collection. They forgot their responsibilities. But when they switched on the radio, they were alarmed to hear the following announcement:

'We interrupt this programme to bring you horrifying news. Two twenty-foot saurians – crocodiles, or perhaps they are alligators – both wearing sunglasses, are driving down the main road in motorized wheelchairs.'

'Oh, no!' cried Archie Lightfoot.

'Oh, no!' cried Marilyn Hawthorn. Together, they ran outside. Their two lawns were quite empty.

'This is serious,' gasped Marilyn. 'Oh, Mr Lightfoot, I must confess that my grandmother is really an alligator!'

'And my old grandfather's a crocodile,' cried Archie. 'I didn't dream that a lovely woman like you could be fond of reptiles.'

'We can discuss that later,' said Marilyn briskly. 'First, we must get our dear pets back.'

Quickly, they climbed into Marilyn's sports car and took off after the runaway reptiles. They soon saw them whizzing along in their wheelchairs. Overhead, a police helicopter hovered, with several policemen and the vet inside it.

'It's very strange,' said Marilyn, 'but they seem to be heading for my uncle's house. I do wish Uncle Hamish were at home. He would know what to do in a case like this.'

The runaways turned into the street where Marilyn's uncle lived, but they did not turn in at his gate. Instead, they went through the next-door gateway, straight to the home of the Reverend Crabtree.

Imagine Marilyn's surprise when she saw her Uncle Hamish sitting on the verandah, showing the Reverend Crabtree his souvenirs of the Orinoco.

'Uncle, I didn't know you were back!' she exclaimed.

'Well, I have only just returned,' he said, looking in amazement at the two reptiles. 'The Orinoco wasn't as good as I remembered it, so I came home early. But Marilyn, why has my alligator split itself in two?'

'Oh, Uncle, this is not another alligator – it's a crocodile. And it belongs to Archie Lightfoot,' Marilyn explained. 'These two bad reptiles ran away together in their wheelchairs and came here.'

By now the police helicopter had landed on the lawn, and the policemen, followed by the vet, came running over.

'Don't hurt those saurians,' the vet was shouting. 'They are not very well. They are in love!'

'Ah,' said the Reverend Crabtree. 'I understand! They have eloped and wish to get married.'

The crocodile and the alligator swished their tails and snapped their jaws as one reptile, to show he was right.

'I'm not sure if I, a minister of the church, should marry an alligator and a crocodile,' said the Reverend Crabtree doubtfully. 'It doesn't seem very respectable.'

'But it seems a pity to miss out on the chance of marrying two creatures so clearly in love,' said Archie. Then, turning to Marilyn he added, 'Suppose we get married, too. Will that make it more respectable? After all, we did bring these two reptiles together. It's only fair that they should do the same for us!'

So Marilyn Hawthorn married Archie Lightfoot, and the crocodile and alligator were married too. Sir Hamish gave both brides away. Then he

swapped over and became best man to the two bridegrooms.

Marilyn and Archie turned their two little houses into one large house, and their lawns into a swimming pool for the two saurians. And they lived happily ever after, even though they had to begin every morning of their lives together feeding sardines to a handsome Nile crocodile and an Orinoco alligator – both with big hearts and even bigger appetites.

Acknowledgements

Every effort has been made to credit correctly the material reproduced in this book. The publishers apologize if any source is wrongly attributed.

'The Family Who Won a Million' © Caroline Castle 1996

'The Family Dog' from *Tales of a Fourth Grade Nothing*, published by The Bodley Head © Judy Blume 1972

'Nothing to Be Afraid Of' from *Nothing to Be Afraid Of*, published by Penguin Books Ltd © Jan Mark 1977, 1980. *The Coronation Mob* was originally commissioned by the BBC in 1977, for the television series 'Jubilee Jackanory', and was published the same year as a book.

'Sniff Finds a Seagull' from *The Sniff Stories*, published by The Bodley Head © Ian Whybrow 1989

'The Pudding Like a Night on the Sea' from *The Julian Stories*, published by Victor Gollancz © Ann Cameron 1981

'Sisterlist' from *The Martians Have Taken My Brother*, published by Hutchinson Children's Books © Rowena Sommerville 1993

'My Gran's Jumper' from *Many Happy Returns*, published by Corgi © Kathryn Cave 1987

'My Dad', published as 'All Right', from *Crummy Mummy and Me*, published by Scholastic Ltd © Anne Fine 1988

'Computer Games' from *Roundabout*, published by Faber and Faber Ltd © Gene Kemp 1993

'The Runaway Reptiles' from *Bubble Trouble*, published by Hamish Hamilton Children's Books © Margaret Mahy 1991